Aesop's (Oh So Slightly) Updated Fables

by Kim Esop-Wylie

Aesop's (Oh So Slightly) Updated Fables was originally produced at the Webster Groves Theatre Guild on December 12th, 1997. The cast was as follows:

```
NARRATOR 1 ........................... Adrienne Doss
DOG .................................. Daniel Hoffman
BUTCHER .............................. Rodney Williams
POND ..................................... Joe Bartell
MISS HARE ........................... Melissa McGiveny
MISS TORTOISE ....................... Shawn Finnegan
NARRATOR 2 ........................... Chris Nausley
GIRL ................................ Maureen Tenant
LOUNGE SINGER ....................... Daniel Hoffman
REPORTER 1 ............................ Molly Downs
REPORTER 2 ........................... Chris Madden
MOUSE ............................... Mallory Reed
LION ................................ Daniel Hoffman
FOX ................................. Rodney Williams
GRAPES .............................. Sarah Headrick
NUMBER BEARER ......................... Nicole Lopez
NARRATOR 3 ........................ Christine Madden
MILLER ........................ Sarah Wickenhauser
SON ...................................... Joe Bartell
DONKEY .............................. Daniel Hoffman
GIRL 2 .............................. Adrienne Doss
GRUMPY OLD GUY ....................... Chris Nausley
WOMAN 1 ............................. Sarah Headrick
WOMAN 2 ............................. Laura Everding
ACTIVIST 1 ............................ Nicole Lopez
ACTIVIST 2 ............................ Molly Downs
NARRATOR 4 ..................... Sarah Wickenhauser
MAID ................................ Laura Everding
CHICKEN 1 ............................ Mallory Reed
CHICKEN 2 ............................ Nicole Lopez
```

For Kate

DOG AND THE BONE

NARRATOR 1
DOG
BUTCHER
GIRL
POND

TORTOISE AND THE HARE

MISS HARE
MISS TORTOISE
NARRATOR 2
GIRL
LOUNGE SINGER

LION AND THE MOUSE

REPORTER 1
REPORTER 2
MOUSE
LION
BUTCHER
GIRL

FOX AND THE GRAPES

FOX
GRAPES
NUMBER BEARER
MISS TORTOISE

THE MILLER, HIS SON, AND THE DONKEY

NARRATOR 3
MILLER
SON
DONKEY
BUTCHER
GIRL
GIRL 2
GRUMPY OLD GUY
WOMAN 1
WOMAN 2
ACTIVIST 1
ACTIVIST 2

THE COUNTRY MAID

NARRATOR 4
MAID
CHICKEN 1
CHICKEN 2
BUTCHER
GIRL

THE DOG AND THE BONE

NARRATOR 1
DOG
BUTCHER
GIRL
POND

NARRATOR. Once upon a time, there was a dirty, scruffy dog. He had dirty fingernails and didn't brush his teeth on a regular basis. And on top of that, he was terribly mean. Oh, yeah, and he was a thief, too. (*Dog growls at Narrator, who coughs, afraid.*) But, uh, other than that, he was a great dog. Great dog.

DOG. (*Swaggering.*) They call me —

NARRATOR. NO! NO, don't say it. I can't stand to hear it!

DOG. You got a problem with my name?

NARRATOR. Oh, um, no. Nope. Your name is very ... descriptive. It's just that it gives me the heebie jeebies.

DOG. (*Skeptically.*) The heebie jeebies?

NARRATOR. Well, just a little.

DOG. That's ok. How about if you don't say my name. In fact, you don't have to saying anything. I'll tell the story and you can just beat it. Just so's you don't get the heebie jeebies. Ok?

NARRATOR. Well, um, see, I'm here to tell the story. (*Laughing nervously.*) That's my job. Um, so, maybe there's a better solution.

DOG. (*Threatening.*) Oh, you don't like my solution?

NARRATOR. No, no, no. See, I just can't say your name, but I still want to be here. Maybe the audience can help. Let's see. What if, everytime what's-his-name's name comes into the story, I pull my nose? And every time I pull my nose, you, the audience, can say his name, you (*To Dog.*) still get to act out the story, and I won't get the heeby jeebies. How about that? Audience, would you help me out? Great! Ok, so once upon a time, there was a dirty, scruffy dog —

DOG. Aren't you forgetting something?

NARRATOR. Let's see. I tied my shoes, and brushed my teeth, and washed behind my ears ...

DOG. (*To audience.*) You guys want to tell him what he forgot? Like, do you even know my name?

NARRATOR. Oh, well, I guess that is a problem. Let's see. Well, what about if you just call him ... Sunshine?

DOG. (*Not happy.*) Sunshine?!

NARRATOR. Or Sparkles? (*Dog growls*) How about Cream Puff? (*Dog growls menacingly*) Or, um, we could call him by his real name, which, is ... (*Narrator shivers with the heeby jeebies.*) Um, his name is ... (*Narrator whispers a name which the audience can't hear.*)

DOG. Huh? (*Narrator whispers a little louder, but still not loud enough.*) HUH?

NARRATOR. SCAB! There! I said it! His name is SCAB! So, everytime I pull my nose, everybody in the audience say, Scab. Ok? So, once upon a time, there was this dog named (*Narrator pulls on his nose and audience says, Scab.*) One day while he was out terrorizing the nice animals of the neighborhood, (*Dog jumps at the audience*) he passed by a butcher's shop, which was run by a very kind and gentle butcher.

BUTCHER. (*Enters scowling.*) I'm a butcher!

NARRATOR. Well, maybe the butcher was having a bad day.

BUTCHER. I cut zings up into little pieces!

NARRATOR. (*Laughing nervously.*) Anyway, when (*Pulls nose.*) passed the butcher's shop, he spied a beautiful, juicy bone sitting on the counter top. And what do you think he did? You guessed it! (*Pulls nose.*) ran into the butcher shop and stole the bone! Well, the, um, kind and gentle butcher tried to reason with the Dog.

BUTCHER. (*Waving a large knife.*) You, Dog! I cut you up into little pieces!

DOG. Only if you catch me! (*Butcher chases Dog offstage.*)

NARRATOR. So, um, the Butcher tried very hard to

have a sincere and calm conversation with the Dog. (*Butcher and Dog run across the stage.*) But, um, it seems that both had a strong inability to communicate their feelings in a constructive way. (*Butcher enters screaming, and Dog barks ferociously. Dog races across the stage, while the Butcher slows down and stops center out of breath.*) Finally, the Dog got so far ahead that the Butcher, who had high blood pressure from all those sausages and what not, knew that the bone was lost forever. But the kind and gentle Butcher accepted defeat with grace and dignity.

GIRL. (*Skips to Butcher and gently tugs his apron.*) La, la, la. Mister, can I have a pound of chopped liver? (*Butcher growls at Girl, waves his knife menacingly, and chases the screaming Girl offstage.*)

NARRATOR. Well, (*Pulls nose.*) ran and ran until he came to a little pond.

POND. (*Less than enthusiastic.*) That's me. The Pond. My mother is so proud. Gee, what part did your kid get? Oh, my kid? Well, my kid is the *Pond.* A very important part. Yup. Very important.

NARRATOR. The Pond seemed to have a little self-esteem problem. But, even though the Pond was small, it was very important to the story. Remember, there aren't any small ponds —

NARRATOR AND POND. Just small pond actors.

POND. Yeah, whatever.

NARRATOR. Right. So, (*Pulls nose.*) stopped at the little, but important, Pond out of breath. And when he looked into the Pond, what do you think he saw? (*Gets responses from the audience.*) That's right! He saw another dog with a bone in his mouth. And that other dog did everything that he did. (*Dog and Pond mimic each other's actions while the Narrator speaks.*) When (*Pulls nose.*) looked sideways, so did the other dog. When (*Pulls nose.*) scratched his ears, so did the other dog. And oh, how juicy and scrumptious that bone looked! Why, it looked almost as good as the bone that (*Pulls nose.*) had stolen from the Butcher! Finally, he couldn't take it any longer! He had to have that other dog's bone! He decided that that other dog's bone looked even juicier and more scrumptious than his own! So, he made up his mind to get that other dog's bone! He looked into the Pond, and then let out a huge growl! (*Dog growls. The bone falls out of his mouth into the Pond, who takes the bone.*)

POND. (*Laughing meanly.*) Ha, ha! Finders keepers. (*Pond exits.*)

NARRATOR. Then (*Pulls nose.*) let out a great howl of anger and frustration. (*Dog howls.*) But the bone was gone forever. What do you think the moral of the story is? (*Talks with audience and then sums it up.*) That's right! Be happy with what you've got! Because if you get too greedy, like (*Pulls nose.*) you could lose everything. (*Dog growls and chases Narrator offstage. Blackout.*)

. . .

THE TORTOISE AND THE HARE

MISS HARE
MISS TORTOISE
NARRATOR 2
GIRL
LOUNGE SINGER

(*Lights up. Girl and Miss Tortoise do warm-up stretches upstage.*)

NARRATOR. (*Wearing an overcoat and hat.*) Hi. I'm Narrator Number Two. But you can call me ... Narrator Number Two. I've got a story to tell. A story with adventure, conflict, romance, and heartbreak. My heartbreak. It all started out on a dark and stormy night. A night like any dark and stormy night. There I was standing in the forest, minding my own business, when she came in ...

HARE. (*Enters wearing aerobic gear.*) OK! Everybody up! We're gonna burn some calories and churn some fat cells! I'm Miss Hare, the fastest aerobics instructor in the West! I'll whip you into shape faster than you can say cellulite! Let's start with some warm-ups! Everybody under the age of ten, stand up and jump with me. That's right! (*Hare gets audience children to stand and jump.*) A one, two, three, four, one, two, three, four ... Now stretch! Good job! Now you can sit down.

NARRATOR. She was a vision in spandex! It was love at first sight! But her love was tougher than a cheap, undercooked pork roast.

HARE. You, there, with the raincoat! I want to see some jumping NOW!

NARRATOR. I didn't know how I got in the class. I didn't even own tennis shoes. Mostly just boots and sandals. But I knew that I loved her more than a tin man loves his oil can. But not everyone loved her style.

TORTOISE. Um, excuse me, but could you slow down

just a little?

HARE. Slow down?! Honey, if you want to slow down, go sit on (*Insert the name of a local congested road.*) at rush hour!

TORTOISE. I just mean that maybe we should be more careful with our heart rates. We don't want to raise them too quickly, do we?

NARRATOR. I agreed with Miss Tortoise, but my heart was already racing.

HARE. You there, in the overcoat! Stop drooling and start jumping! (*Hare jumps over to Narrator and smacks him on the rear.*)

NARRATOR. (*Happily.*) Our aerobics class lasted five wonderful hours. I ached like a cat without a litter box. But I had to talk to her ... Excuse me, Miss Hare?

HARE. Talk fast. I have another class in ten minutes.

NARRATOR. Miss Hare, I, um, didn't understand that one move you did? The heal, kick up, something, something, something?

HARE. (*Demonstrating quickly.*) Heel, toe, up, side together side?

NARRATOR. Yeah, that's the one! Could you maybe show it to me? In private?

HARE. Can't. Got another class. Maybe next time. Ta ta! (*She exits.*)

NARRATOR. I was crushed like a penny on a railroad track.

TORTOISE. (*Crossing to him.*) What's wrong?

NARRATOR. I ... I'm crushed like a penny on a railroad track, like a bird with no depth perception, like a —

TORTOISE. Like an egg under a cement truck? (*Narrator and Tortoise turn to one another and share a love struck look. Lounge Singer enters singing into his thumb and stepping between the two.*)

LOUNGE SINGER. The Love Boat ... La la la la la la la la laaaa. The Love Boat ... I don't know the rest of the words to this song ... (*Lounge Singer makes a cheesy shooting gesture to the audience and backs offstage trying not to look like an idiot, but failing miserably.*)

TORTOISE. Here, let me help. Stand like this. Now, first put your toe on the floor like this. That's right. Now put your heel down. Good. Now step side, now put your feet together, and now step to the side again. Excellent! Sometimes it just pays to go a little slower, that's all.

NARRATOR. Yes! Yes, that's it! When Miss Hare came in, so fast and furious, I thought —

TORTOISE. Yes?

NARRATOR. I fell in love with her speed, her flare, her pace! But suddenly, I'm thinking that maybe I want to slow down a little.

TORTOISE. Yes, I agree. Slow is better. Gosh, I really like you. Too bad we'll never see each other again.

NARRATOR. What?

TORTOISE. I'm quitting this class. It's just not for me.

HARE. (*Enters jumping.*) Ok, class. Let's start with a few jumping jacks, say, two hundred? Let's go! Hey, you two! I said, let's go!

TORTOISE. (*To Narrator.*) Good-bye.

NARRATOR. Wait!

HARE. You! In the overcoat! Two hundred jumping jacks! NOW!

NARRATOR. No, wait! (*Narrator runs after Tortoise, bumping into her, who then bumps into Girl, who then bumps into Hare. All fall on the floor.*)

HARE. (*To Girl.*) Watch it, Lard Foot! (*Girl cries loudly and exits in tears.*)

HARE. Whoa, whoa, whoa! Take five everybody. What's going on here? You, Miss Tortoise? You're not nearly physically fit enough to be causing this much trouble.

TORTOISE. I really need for you to be less rude, Miss Hare.

HARE. Rude? Baby, you ain't even seen rude.

TORTOISE. And neither have you.

NARRATOR. (*To audience.*) Would you believe it? The two females of my dreams were about to have a cat fight! I was as giddy as a —

HARE. Oh yeah? Listen Baby Pudge, come back and

fight when you have a little more muscle.

NARRATOR. You tell her! (*Tortoise throws him a quizzical look.*)

TORTOISE. I'll have you know that I happen to have more muscle than ninety-three percent of the turtles in this region.

NARRATOR. Yeah! So there! (*Hare throws him a quizzical look.*)

HARE. Prove it.

TORTOISE. Gladly. How about a little race?

HARE. My pleasure. How about a mile?

TORTOISE. How about five?

HARE. Five miles? Piece of cake.

TORTOISE. Really? Then let's make it ten.

HARE. You're on. You in the overcoat. Start us.

NARRATOR. And there they were. The two most opposite and perfect creatures I'd ever met. I felt like a dryer sheet in the spin cycle, like a kernel in a popcorn machine, like a —

HARE. GO! (*Hare races offstage. Tortoise calmly walks after her but stops to blow the Narrator a kiss. He watches the kiss slowly arc through the air and then catches it.*)

NARRATOR. Oh, yeaaahhhh.

GIRL. (*Enters to center.*) And the moral of the story is —

NARRATOR. Wait a minute, wait a minute! You can't tell the moral! The story's not even over yet! Telling the moral now would be like, like eating the chocolate bunny ears the night before Easter! It'd be like getting a grade before you took the test! It'd be like ... Aww heck, it would just be really doofy!

GIRL. (*Dissolving into tears.*) Waaaaaa! (*Runs offstage.*)

NARRATOR. (*Impressed.*) Can I make 'em run or what? (*Blackout.*)

. . .

THE LION AND THE MOUSE

REPORTERS 1 and 2
MOUSE
LION
BUTCHER
GIRL

(Lights up. Reporters are heard offstage loudly asking questions. Mouse runs across stage terrified, chased by Reporters.)

REPORTER 1. Is it true, Miss Mouse?
REPORTER 2. How close were you to the lion's teeth?
REPORTER 1. Did he have bad breath?
MOUSE. *(Bashfully.)* Gee, I, uh, don't remember.
REPORTER 2. Is it true that Hollywood wants the rights to your story?
REPORTER 1. Will you be writing a book?
REPORTER 2. How many talk shows do you have lined up?
MOUSE. *(Flustered.)* I, I, I, IYYIYIYIYIYIYI!

(Mouse exits screaming. Reporters run after her. Mouse returns to the empty stage, making sure that no one has followed her.)

Is the coast clear? Do you see any reporters? Good! Well, hi, there. I'm Mouse or Miss Mouse if you want to be formal. But I don't mind what you call me. Just Mouse is fine. Golly, have you ever had a reporter follow you? At first you'd think it would be fun being famous and all. But then, they never leave you alone. Why, you can't even scratch your nose without somebody snooping around to catch a peek. *(Reporters are heard offstage.)* Quick, hide me! *(Mouse runs into the audience and hides. Reporters enter and ask the audience rapid-fire questions.)*
REPORTER 1. Have you seen a mouse, yeah high, yeah

tall, with big ears?

REPORTER 2. Where did she go? Was anyone with her? Were they in a car? What color was the car?

REPORTER 1. They were in a car? Oh, a train? No, a purple helicopter with orange wheels? And you say they were going to France to buy toothpicks?

REPORTER 2. I'm not a bit surprised. Let's go! (*Reporters exit.*)

MOUSE. (*Coming back on stage.*) Gee, thanks for getting rid of them! I owe you one! You know, that's really what this whole thing is about. When someone does something nice for someone else. It all started out when I was walking through the woods one day, minding my own business and singing my favorite song, the theme to Mission Impossible. (*Mouse dances around stage humming the Mission Impossible theme song.*) And I was so busy singing and dancing that I didn't even know I had entered the place of the Great Lion, the scariest, hungriest, most ferocious lion in the whole world! And just when I realized that I was in the place of the Great Lion, I felt warm breath on my shoulder. (*Lion enters and saunters to Mouse, breathing loudly and ominously over her.*) And how do you think I felt then? (*Waits for audience to respond and then whispers.*) You're right! I was just a teeny, weenie bit afraid! (*Lion makes smacking noises and pulls out a plastic knife and fork and then tucks a napkin under his neck.*) And then, from out of nowhere, it occurred to me that the Great Lion was going to eat me! And then you know what else I realized? I realized that I really didn't *want* the Great Lion to eat me! Yeah, it surprised me, too! And just when I felt the lion's mouth right next to my head, I said something so original that it stopped the Lion in mid-bite! (*Turns to Lion and screams.*) ANALGESIC!

LION. (*Calmly.*) I beg your pardon?

MOUSE. ANALGESIC!

LION. Yes, I heard it the first time.

MOUSE. ANALGESIC!!!!!!!!! It means a drug that takes away pain, like aspirin.

LION. Yes, I am aware of what the word means. I am, however, curious as to why you would say it just as I'm about to bite you in half.

MOUSE. Well, you see, I really have a terrible skin problem, and I'm afraid that if you eat me, that little pieces of my skin will get all mixed up with your beautiful, golden skin, and then you'll end up with the very same skin problem.

LION. (*Interested.*) I see. And what if I should eat you anyway and not get your terrible skin problem?

MOUSE. Oh, well, that's where the analgesic comes in. See, even if you don't really get my terrible skin problem, you'll probably still be thinking about that terrible skin problem? Am I right?

LION. Perhaps. Do go on.

MOUSE. Well, so let's just say that you don't get the skin problem. But there you are, days later, thinking about it, wondering, My goodness, even though I gobbled up that little mouse with the terrible skin problem, I don't seem to have gotten any terrible skin problem on my own beautiful, golden skin. But then you think, What if I should get that terrible skin problem tomorrow? So you wait until the next day and then you see a little flake of skin, and then you worry that the terrible skin problem has finally arrived. But maybe not. It could just be a little flake of skin, just minding its own business. So then you spend all your time thinking is it or isn't it, is it or isn't it. And then you start spending all your time worrying about it and you stop doing all the things you really enjoy, like bowling (*Lion mimics throwing a bowling ball.*) and flying kites (*Lion mimics flying a kite.*) and practicing your favorite song like this. (*Both Lion and Mouse dance as Mouse hums the Mission Impossible theme song.*) And then your family is so worried about you that they stop doing all the things that they like to do, and by then everyone is so worried and upset and can't get any sleep that they all have big, huge headaches and the only solution then is an —

LION. Analgesic.

MOUSE. You bet your sweet bippy! (*Mouse punches Lion in the arm and then pats the arm apologetically.*) Oh, Great Lion, Sir. (*To audience.*) And then you know what the Lion did? No, he didn't eat me! He laughed! He laughed a great, big, giant lion laugh!

LION. (*Laughing.*) Well, I must say, this is quite original.

MOUSE. Really? I am?

LION. Oh, yes. I've eaten quite a few animals in my day, and usually they say the most mundane things. For example, "Don't eat me, please don't eat me." When I hear that, I'm required to eat the poor beast, even if I'm not especially hungry. You see, I feel it's my duty to rid the earth of boring beings. But, you, my little friend, you have said something no one else has ever dared to say.

LION AND MOUSE. Analgesic.

LION. So, I congratulate you. And because of your originality, even despite the fact that I'm a tad bit hungry, I release you. Go on your way, little mouse. And continue to be original. The world could use much more of that.

MOUSE. And so, just like that, the Great Lion let me go. And I started to run away really fast, when I remembered something my mama told me. She said that when you meet a very great, very important person, you should always bow. So, I stopped, and even though I was still kind of afraid, I knew that the Great Lion was one of those very great, very important people my mama told me about. (*Mouse tiptoes back to Lion and slowly bows.*) And then I ran really fast! Golly, I've never been so surprised in my whole life! That Lion could have swallowed me whole, but for some reason, he spared my life. And I thought that was the end of the story until a couple of weeks later, when there was a big commotion all throughout the forest.

REPORTER 1. (*Briskly enters with Reporter 2*) Did you hear? Oh, my, my, my, my, my! They say he put up a tremendous struggle!

REPORTER 2. You don't say? Well, I heard that he has

to have fourteen hundred nets just to keep him still! They say that he's going to be roasted in a celebration that will feed the whole city!

REPORTER 1. Roasted?!

REPORTERS 1 AND 2. Yummy, yummy, yum! (*Reporters exit.*)

MOUSE. And at first I didn't know what they were talking about, until I heard it. It was terrible. The saddest, most heartbreaking sound I'd ever heard. (*Butcher enters pulling Lion in a wagon. Lion sits sadly wrapped in netting.*)

LION. (*Roars a great, sad roar.*) Roaarrrrrrrrrr!

BUTCHER. (*Stops to sharpen big carving knife.*) You, Lion, be kviet! Or I cut you up into little pieces! Vell, I vill cut you up into little pieces anyvay! Ha, ha, ha, ha, ha ... (*Exits laughing.*)

MOUSE. And there he was, the Great Lion! My Great Lion! The Lion that thought I was so original. The Lion that spared my life when he could have crunched me like a potato chip! So, I made up my mind! I was going to free that Lion, even if it cost me my life. I started chewing on the netting, and chewing, and chewing, and chewing. My gums got sore, my teeth bled, my tongue got rope burn. But I kept chewing! And finally, I chewed a hole just big enough for the Great Lion. (*To Lion.*) Run, run, run! (*Girl enters singing and skipping across the stage and bumps into Lion. She stares in shock at Lion, screams in terror, and exits. Butcher and Reporters are heard offstage.*)

MOUSE. RUN!

(*Lion begins to run offstage, then stops and turns slowly back to Mouse. Lion walks slowly back to Mouse and bows gracefully. Lion then bounds away. Butcher and Reporters enter and see that Lion is gone. All run after Lion with great commotion.*)

Did you see that? Did you see it? Golly, he bowed. The

Great Lion bowed! To me?! Golllleeee. I keep thinking that there's got to be a lesson here, but I'm just not sure what it is. What do you think? (*Asks audience to come up with the moral.*) You know, I think you're right. When you do something nice, whether it's for a real big person like the Lion or a small person like me, that nice thing is never a waste. Yup, I think you're right.

GIRL. (*Enters, points at Mouse and screams.*) That Mouse! That Mouse let the Lion go! I saw the whole thing! (*Butcher and Reporters are heard offstage.*)

MOUSE. Oops, gotta go. Hey, I know! Create a diversion! Everyone do this! (*Sings and dances to the Mission Impossible theme.*) Come on! Everybody! Thanks! (*Mouse gets audience singing and dancing. Butcher and Reporters enter just as Mouse sneaks out through the audience. Butcher and Reporters exit chasing her. Blackout.*)

• • •

FOX AND THE GRAPES

FOX
GRAPES
NUMBER BEARER
MISS TORTOISE

> (*Lights up. Grapes is perched high on a stool filing her nails.*)

GRAPES. (*Bored.*) Oh, hi. I didn't see you there. But now I do. Ha ha. My name is Hybrid Number three-five-eight-one-four, a highly flavored, completely seedless grape introduced in 1977 by the New York Agricultural Experiment Station. But you can call me Grapes. Everybody does. Well, ok, they don't just call me Grapes. They really call me The Most Scrumptious, Delicious, Intensely Perfect Grape that ever grew on the planet, blah blah blah. I guess you could say I'm kind of famous. (*Sighs heavily.*) But being perfect is just so borrrrrinnnnnngggggggg. I wish I weren't intensely perfect! I wish I were just a normal, everyday, not-so-famous or scrumptious, or delicious, or intensely perfect grape! (*Sighs heavily.*) What I wouldn't give for a little excitement.

FOX. (*Swaggers in.*) Hello? Did someone call? Fox is my name, excitement is my game!

GRAPES. Oh, look. A little varmint.

FOX. Oh, look! Scrumptious, delicious, grapes!

GRAPES. You forgot intensely perfect.

FOX. Oh, yes. Intensely perfect! So, what's a nice scrumptious, delicious, intensely perfect grape like you doing on a vine like this?

GRAPES. Oh, nothing. Just being intensely perfect.

FOX. (*Licking his chops.*) Sounds quite appetizing.

GRAPES. Not really. It's actually rather stressful being so intensely perfect all the time.

FOX. Oh, you poor thing! Why don't you come down

here, and I'll rub your neck?

GRAPES. No thanks.

FOX. How about a foot massage?

GRAPES. I don't think so.

FOX. How about a fang rub?

GRAPES. A fang rub? What's that?

FOX. Why, you've never heard of a fang rub? Of all the ... My girl, where have you been? It's the latest craze! Of course, it's very expensive, and only the very scrumptious, the very delicious, the very perfect can safely undergo the treatment.

GRAPES. Well, I certainly qualify. What do I do?

FOX. That's the beauty of it. You don't do anything! I do all the work. First I carefully remove you from the vine. Then I gently rub off the debris and dirt. You know, get rid of all that dead skin and bring out the underlying beauty. Then I gently rub you with my fangs to bring out that oh-so-yummy-grape glow!

GRAPES. It won't hurt will it? Because one time I had a facial and it made my skin all puckery. I looked like a raisin for two whole days! And in addition to looking simply awful, it hurt.

FOX. Oh, no, Sweet Grape, I guarantee that it won't hurt (*Whispers aside.*) me.

GRAPES. So how much will this treatment cost?

FOX. Oh, Sweet Grapes, why would I want to charge you when you are doing me a favor? You see, my time on this earth is running short.

GRAPES. You mean you're dying?

FOX. Yes, (*Aside.*) of starvation.

GRAPES. Oh, you poor thing. Well, if it would make you happy, then of course you can give me a fang rub.

FOX. Hello dinner!

GRAPES. What did you say?

FOX. Mellow winner! I always say that to those lucky enough to get my wonderful fang rub!

GRAPES. Oh. Now, you're going to have to jump just a little to reach my stem.

FOX. No problem, Sweet Grape! (*Aside.*) Prepare to

meet your maker.

GRAPES. What?

FOX. I said prepare to fleet our taker. It's just something we foxes say. Here I come! (*Fox charges toward Grapes, leaps awkwardly and misses. Number Bearer enters and displays a sign awarding the leap a score of 9.5. Fox growls at Number Bearer, who then scurries away.*)

GRAPES. 9.5 —Not bad. This time keep your hind leg bent just a bit more.

FOX. Like this? (*Bending leg.*)

GRAPES. Perfect. (*Fox leaps again, this time a little more awkwardly. He again misses Grapes. Number Bearer enters and displays a score of 7.2. Fox growls and chases Number Bearer away.*)

GRAPES. No, no, no. Your form is all wrong. Think like a bird. Use your arms to float you.

FOX. My arms?

GRAPES. To float.

FOX. To float.

GRAPES. Think like a bird. You know, soar.

FOX. (*Aside.*) That's what you're going to be after I take a bite out of you.

GRAPES. Could you speak up a little?

FOX. I said I'd gladly soar for you, Sweet Grapes! Let me try again.

GRAPES. Remember, bend your leg. Lift your arms. Soar like a dove. (*Fox takes a running leap, flies awkwardly, and crashes into Tortoise, who slowly crosses the stage.*) Hmm. That looked more like a frog than a dove. (*Tortoise calmly gets up, dusts herself off, and hands Fox a slip of paper.*)

FOX. What's this?

TORTOISE. A citizen's arrest. For jumping like a frog in an unauthorized area.

FOX. (*Threateningly.*) Why you — (*Tortoise calmly holds up a finger, in effect telling Fox to wait just a moment. She slowly takes out a long metal tube.*) What's that?

Tortoise. A cattle prod. (*Tortoise touches Fox with tube. Fox yelps in pain. Tortoise exits slowly while Grapes laughs loudly.*)

Fox. (*Very angry.*) Why you ... you ... You aren't sweet at all!

Grapes. No, not really. But then, you aren't quite as smart as you think you are, are you?

Fox. You! You're a sour, sour Grape! Do you hear me?! Sour, sour, SOUR!

Grapes. Sticks and stones may break my bones, but names will never hurt me because I'm scrumptious and delicious and intensely perfect, and you're, well ... not.

Fox. I didn't want to give you a fang rub anyway, you pucker skinned, full of seeds, mushy on one side, grimy stemmed sour-like-a-Sweet-Tart Grape! (*Fox exits in a huff.*)

Grapes. Well, what do you make of that?

Number Bearer. (*Enters.*) People pretend to hate what they can't have. Thank you. (*Blackout.*)

. . .

THE MILLER, HIS SON, AND THE DONKEY

NARRATOR
MILLER
SON
DONKEY
BUTCHER
GIRL 1
GIRL 2
GRUMPY OLD GUY
WOMAN 1
WOMAN 2
ACTIVIST 1
ACTIVIST 2

(*Lights up.*)

NARRATOR. Once upon a time, there was a Miller, (*Miller enters and salutes.*) his Son, (*Son enters and waves stupidly.*) and their Donkey. (*Donkey enters heeing and hawing. Butcher also enters.*) Uh, excuse, me, but did I say there was a Butcher?

BUTCHER. Vell, no, but you never know vhen you vill need a butcher vith a big knife.

NARRATOR. That's very true. However, this story doesn't really need a butcher or a big knife.

BUTCHER. No big knife? Are you sure? You don't have any cutting up into little pieces?

NARRATOR. No, no cutting into little pieces. Not in this story. But thanks anyway.

BUTCHER. You vill call me if you need cutting up into little pieces?

NARRATOR. You're the first on my list.

BUTCHER. Ok Bye. (*Exits.*)

NARRATOR. As I was saying, the Miller needed some cash, so he decided to sell his Donkey. (*Donkey brays.*) Yeah, yeah, life's rough. So, the Miller, his Son, and the Donkey set out to the village where the Donkey could be sold. (*Miller hangs a "for sale" sign on Donkey, who brays in protest. All three walk the stage in a large circle.*) On the way into the village, the three passed a group of girls playing along side the road.

GIRL 1. Ha ha! Look at that!

GIRL 2. Yeah, look at that!

NARRATOR. The girls were just a tiny bit rude and twerpy.

GIRL 1. Hey, Mister! Like, nice donkey!

GIRL 2. Yeah, nice donkey!

GIRL. Everybody knows that if you have a donkey, you're supposed to ride him! That's what donkeys are for! Duh!

GIRL 2. Yeah. Duh!

NARRATOR. And the Miller listened to the rude, twerpy girls and decided that they were right. So, he hauled his Son onto the Donkey (*Donkey brays.*). Yeah, yeah, we hear you. So, on they went. And a little while later, they came upon an Grumpy Old Guy talking to himself by the side of the road.

GRUMPY OLD GUY. Cheeseballs, that's what I tell 'em. Computers really run on CHEESEBALLS! Big, puffy, orange cheeseballs. With nuts on top!

NARRATOR. The Miller, his Son, and the Donkey felt sorry for the Grumpy Old Guy, so they stopped to offer him some of their roast beef sandwiches.

BUTCHER. (*Peeking in.*) Vhich I vill cut!

NARRATOR. (*Playing along.*) Which the Butcher cut. (*Butcher enters. Son hands over the sandwich, which the Butcher cuts.*)

SON. Gee, Mister, you sure are some cutter upper.

BUTCHER. (*Puffing up his chest with butchery pride.*) My vork here is done. (*Butcher exits.*)

NARRATOR. But the Grumpy Old Guy didn't want their sandwiches.

GRUMPY OLD GUY. (*Throwing sandwiches.*) I'm not hungry! I'm Jesus!

SON. Cool! Are you really Jesus?

GRUMPY OLD GUY. Yes, I am. Or I'm that one other guy that plays basketball.

SON. You mean Michael Jordan? You're Michael Jordan? Dad, Dad! Look, it's Michael Jordan!

GRUMPY OLD GUY. Yeah, that's who I am. But I don't want any of your stinky sandwiches because you have no respect for your elders. What's wrong with you anyway?! You got cheeseballs in your brain?! Why don't you let your old man ride? You oughta be ashamed! Big, healthy boy like you! You'll never make the NBA with that attitude!

SON. *(Begins to cry.)* Daaaaddd!

NARRATOR. So, the Miller decided that the Grumpy Old Guy was right, and that he should ride and the Son should walk. (*Old Man pulls Son off Donkey and gets on Donkey. Donkey brays loudly.*)

SON. (*Upset having to walk.*) Daaaaaddd!

NARRATOR. Yeah, yeah. We hear your pain. So they continued on their way to the village, and the Grumpy Old Guy decided to tag along, which would have been okay, except that the Grumpy Old Guy liked to sing.

GRUMPY OLD GUY. (*Singing.*) Doo bee doo bee dooo ...

SON. (*Covering his ears.*) Daaaaddd!

NARRATOR. And soon they passed a group of women out chatting.

WOMAN 1. Did you hear? My uncle's half brother on my mother's side twice removed is going to marry my second cousin's niece's daughter on my father's side! Oy!

WOMAN 2. Well, would you look at that! A perfectly healthy adult riding a donkey while that poor child has to walk. You, boy, come here! You poor thing! (*Woman hugs Son, against his will.*)

SON. (*Alarmed.*) DAAAADDD!

WOMAN 1. See this boy? He's miserable! That's child abuse, don't you know, that's just what it is! Child abuse! I'm calling the Division of Family Services! They'll put you in jail, Mister, for making that poor, abused boy walk while you ride high and mighty on your mule!

DONKEY. Donkey!

WOMAN 1 AND 2. Who asked you?

NARRATOR. So, the Miller decided that not only was

the Grumpy Old Guy right, but so were the women. So, he hauled his Son on top of the Donkey with him, and they both rode on the Donkey into the village. (*Donkey brays loudly.*) Yeah, yeah. I know. Two's a load. So, they continued on their journey until they happened upon a group of people yelling and carrying signs.

ACTIVIST 1. DON'T HURT THE BUNNIES, DON'T HURT THE BUNNIES!

ACTIVIST 2. FUR IS SOMEBODY'S SKIN! HOW WOULD YOU LIKE IT IF SOMEBODY WANTED TO WEAR YOUR SKIN?!

ACTIVIST 1. REAL MEN DON'T HUNT! REAL MEN DON'T HUNT!

GRUMPY OLD GUY. (*Joining the Activists.*) DON'T EAT THE CHEESEBALLS! DON'T EAT THE CHEESEBALLS!

ACTIVIST 2. Hey, look at that! That man and that boy are both riding on that poor, abused donkey! Hey, you, Mister! You ought to be ashamed!

MILLER. Whatever for?

ACTIVIST 1. For abusing the rights of a mule!

DONKEY. Donkey!

ACTIVIST 1 AND 2. Who asked you?

MILLER. Please let us through. We've come a long way and we're tired. We're just on our way to the village to sell the Donkey.

ACTIVIST 1. (*Speaking into walkie talkie.*) Code Blue, Code Blue. We have a situation here. Inhumane selling of livestock. Repeat, inhumane selling of livestock!

MILLER. But you don't understand. My whole family is going hungry! We must eat!

ACTIVIST 2. Oh, DEAR LORD, HE'S GOING TO EAT THE MULE! ALERT, ALERT! (*Spins in place and makes a siren sound.*)

ACTIVIST 1. You are in deep, deep trouble! You, Mister, you are going to jail! And you, Son, you are going far, far away to a home for bad boys who are cruel to animals!

SON. (*Screaming.*) DAAAAAAADDD!

GRUMPY OLD GUY. Hey, what about me?

ACTIVIST 2. You're getting some singing lessons,

Grandpa!

MILLER. Wait, wait! Look, what can I do to stop this?

ACTIVIST 2. Well, there's only one way to undo the damage you've done.

MILLER. What? Please tell me! I'll do anything!

ACTIVIST 1. You'll have to kiss the donkey's hooves and beg for his forgiveness.

DONKEY. (*Brays in agreement.*) Finally, a little respect.

MILLER. All right, I'll do it. (*Miller kisses Donkey's hoof. Donkey holds a hoof up for Son to kiss.*)

SON. (*Protesting.*) Daaaaddd!

DONKEY. (*Whispering to Son.*) Wiener. (*Donkey then holds up a hoof for Grumpy Old Guy, who takes the hoof, gladly.*)

GRUMPY OLD GUY. You know how long it's been since I got to smooch a donkey foot? (*Passionately kisses the Donkey's hoof until Donkey, braying in protest, is able to pull it away.*)

MILLER. Are we done here?

ACTIVIST 2. No way, Jose. Now you'll have to carry him home.

MILLER AND SON. Carry him?

DONKEY. (*Snorts in laughter.*) Hot diggity!

ACTIVIST 1. Kind of like he's a king, and you two are his servants.

MILLER. And this is the only way to avoid trouble with the law?

ACTIVIST 1 AND 2. The only way.

NARRATOR. So, with much groaning and straining, the Miller and his Son hoisted the Donkey into the air. And the people of the village watched the odd sight and laughed and laughed and laughed. (*Girls, Women, Butcher, and Activists laugh heartily.*) The Miller and his Son got maybe ten feet when they both lost their balance and dropped the Donkey off the side of the road which happened to be a really steep cliff that was about a thousand foot drop. (*Donkey brays in refusal.*) Hey, sorry, Donkey dude, but that's how the story goes. (*Miller and the Son reluctantly play out the fall. The Donkey rolls offstage and brays a long, drifting scream.)*

SON. DAAAAAADDD!

MILLER. (*Losing his temper.*) WHHAAAAAATTT????!!!

SON. Can we go home now?

NARRATOR. And so the Miller and his Son slowly walked home, while the Grumpy Old Guy went on to Branson, Missouri to be lead singer in the Cheeseball Quartet.

GRUMPY OLD GUY. (*Excited.*) Doo bee doo bee doooo ... (*He exits.*)

NARRATOR. The Miller and his Son trudged home tired and hungry, but most of all they were embarrassed. They lost their Donkey and everyone in the whole village was laughing. (*All laugh at Miller and his Son.*)

GIRL. What a putz!

GIRL 2. Yeah, what a putz!

NARRATOR. You see, he who tries to please everyone, pleases no one. (*Narrator exits. Hare enters panting and stops to look offstage where Donkey rolled.*)

HARE. Hey, you! Donkey in the ditch! You'll never reach your target heartrate just lying there with your legs up in the air like that! (*Donkey brays weakly.*) Hey, I know what you need! You need some coffee! I myself drink at least twenty-three cups a day. I'm never low on energy! I'll give you a sip of mine, okay? (*Hare opens her thermos and screams.*) OH, MY GOD! My coffee! It's ... GONE! My energy, it's ... melting. Melting ... My precious energy, it's ... (*Hare falls to the floor and snores loudly. Butcher enters and spies the sleeping Hare. He giggles happily and wakes her up.*) Hey. Do you have any coffee?

BUTCHER. Coffee? Oh, yes, ve have lots and lots of coffee.

HARE. Oh, good.

BUTCHER. Yes, coffee is very very good. Vith rabbit stew! (*Hare suddenly looks closely at Butcher and his large knife, and exits, running. Butcher chases her and exits. Blackout.*)

. . .

THE COUNTRY MAID

NARRATOR 4
MAID
CHICKEN 1
CHICKEN 2
BUTCHER
MISS TORTOISE
GIRL

(*Lights up.*)

NARRATOR. Once upon a time, there was a cheerful young woman who loved animals.

MAID. (*Very enthusiastic but not very bright.*) I love aminals!

NARRATOR. She loved big animals and small animals, brown animals, purple animals, animals of all shapes and sizes and colors. But most of all, more than any other animal, the young woman loved ...

MAID. (*Wildly.*) CHICKENS! I LOVE CHICKENS! Chickens are my most favorite, special, wonderful aminal! What's your most favorite, special wonderful aminal? (*Discusses with the audience.*) That's nice. I love chickens best.

NARRATOR. The young woman loved chickens so much that she decided to raise chickens in her spare time. So she bought two chickens. (*Chickens enter clucking and sit.*)

MAID. Oh, goody! Chickens! Two perfect little chickens!

NARRATOR. And the young woman encouraged them to lay lots of eggs.

MAID. Come on, Chickies! Lay those eggs! Come on!

CHICKEN 1. Easy for you to say! Balk, balk, balk.

CHICKEN 2. Come on, little Chickies! You can do it!

NARRATOR. And then the chickens laid two perfect little eggs. The young woman picked up the eggs and began to dream of the future.

CHICKEN 1. Did you see that? Not even a thank you!

MAID. Just think. If these two chickens laid twenty more eggs, (*Chickens balk.*) or fifty eggs, (*Chickens balk louder.*) Or one hundred eggs ... (*Chickens balk manaically.*) Gosh! And if those hundred eggs hatch, and then those hundred eggs lay twenty more eggs ... (*Chickens continue to balk.*)

CHICKEN 1. No room! No room!

MAID. Or if those hundred chickens lay fifty eggs —

CHICKEN 2. No more! No more!

MAID. Or if those hundred chickens lay another hundred eggs and then all two hundred chickens lay another two hundred eggs ... (*Chickens flap around in a circle, extremely upset.*) Gosh, what would I do with all those chickens?

BUTCHER. I know vhat to do vith chickens! (*Chickens run to Maid and hide behind her, squawking loudly.*)

MAID. NOOOOOOOOO!!! Go away, you, you, cutter upper! My chickens are not for you!

BUTCHER. Humph! (*Butcher starts to exit in a huff, but stops as Tortoise enters. He eyes her hungrily.*) My favorite! Turtle soup! Come here, yummy little turtle! (*Tortoise inches away. Butcher runs toward her. Tortoise raises a ringer to say, in effect, "Wait just a moment." Then she calmly takes out her can of mace and sprays him in the face. She exits as Butcher yelps in pain and staggers offstage. Chickens salute Tortoise as she exits.*)

MAID. My goodness, in just two months these two little eggs could easily become ... (*Takes out a calculator and punches in some numbers.*) ... twenty-three thousand, four hundred and fifty eggs! And I'll bet I could sell them for about five cents each, so that would be ...

NARRATOR. One thousand one hundred seventy-two dollars and fifty cents!

MAID. Wow wee! That ain't chicken feed! Boy, I could do a lot with one thousand, one hundred seventy-two dollars and fifty cents! Why, I could buy a new house for my chickens! (*Chickens cluck happily.*) Or I could stock up on chicken feed! (*Chickens cluck more happily.*) Or I could even buy some little itty bitty clothes and dress 'em up and have a little chicken fashion show! (*Chickens are about to cluck happily, but then sigh in disappointment.*) Gosh, what would you do if you had one thousand, one hundred seventy-two dollars and fifty cents? (*Maid talks with the audience about what they would do with the money.*)

NARRATOR. But soon the young Maid wasn't even thinking about where she was going and before she knew it … (*Girl runs onto stage skipping and singing and bumps into the Maid, who then drops both of her eggs. Girl, Maid, and Chickens sob loudly.*) And there you have it, ladies and gentlemen. Whatever you do, don't count your chickens before they hatch! (*Blackout.*)

(*Lights up. Narrator 2 enters and unravels a strip of paper on the floor.*)

NARRATOR 2. Hi, it's me. Narrator Number Two. Well, here's the ten mile finish line. Have you seen Miss Tortoise or Miss Hare? Where could they be? (*Tortoise enters dragging in Hare, who is fast asleep.*) And then my heart stopped faster than a zit appears before a big date! Miss Hare was dead!

TORTOISE. Not dead, just in a caffeine slump. She should wake up in a few hours. And I've taken the liberty to set up a doctor's appointment for her. She needs some advice for how to change her fast-paced lifestyle.

NARRATOR 2. What concern! What compassion! What strong arms! And that's when I knew, like a shoe salesman knows foot corns, that Miss Tortoise was the turtle for me. (*Kneeling in front of Tortoise.*) Miss Tortoise, would you, could you, might you consider being my bride? Or at least my pet?

TORTOISE. Now, now, not so fast. Over the course of this ten mile race, I have become terribly fond of you. But why don't we just take it slow and give our love some time to grow?

NARRATOR 2. And she can rhyme! Ladies and gentlemen, that's when I saw the truth! Slow and steady wins the race! And my heart!

TORTOISE. And the guy. (*Tortoise and Narrator 2 book arms and exit just as Hare wakes up and inches herself to the finish line.*)

HARE. I won! I won! I — (*She falls alseep again. Blackout.*)

. . .

No one shall make any changes in this title(s) for the purpose of production. No part of this book may be reproduced, stored in a retrieval system, scanned, uploaded, or transmitted in any form, by any means, now known or yet to be invented, including mechanical, electronic, digital, photocopying, recording, videotaping, or otherwise, without the prior written permission of the publisher. No one shall share this title(s), or any part of this title(s), through any social media or file hosting websites.

For all inquiries regarding motion picture, television, online/digital and other media rights, please contact Concord Theatricals Corp.

MUSIC AND THIRD-PARTY MATERIALS USE NOTE

Licensees are solely responsible for obtaining formal written permission from copyright owners to use copyrighted music and/or other copyrighted third-party materials (e.g. artworks, logos) in the performance of this play and are strongly cautioned to do so. If no such permission is obtained by the licensee, then the licensee must use only original music and materials that the licensee owns and controls. Licensees are solely responsible and liable for clearances of all third-party copyrighted materials, including without limitation music, and shall indemnify the copyright owners of the play(s) and their licensing agent, Concord Theatricals Corp., against any costs, expenses, losses and liabilities arising from the use of such copyrighted third-party materials by licensees. For music, please contact the appropriate music licensing authority in your territory for the rights to any incidental music.

IMPORTANT BILLING AND CREDIT REQUIREMENTS

If you have obtained performance rights to this title, please refer to your licensing agreement for important billing and credit requirements.